This book belongs to

....

Devised by Joanna Bicknell.

Written by Nick Page.

Illustrations by Tim Hutchinson.

Mice by Jo Bishop, Caroline Hart and Carole Meredith.

Designed by Annie Simpson.

Photography by Andy Snaith.

Research by Hayley Down.

Copyright © 2013

make believe ideas ltd

The Wilderness, Berkhamsted, Hertfordshire, HP4 2AZ, UK.
565 Royal Parkway, Nashville, TN 37214, USA.

www.makebelieveideas.com

MOUSETON ABBEY

THE MISSING DIAMOND

Joanna Bicknell · Nick Page

make
believe
ideas

MOUSETON ABBEY

A BRIEF HISTORY

Mouseton Abbey was built some time around 1297 – Thursday, teatime. As an abbey, it was originally home to the monastic mice of The Stinky Brotherhood of the Holey Goatscheese, but by 1473, the house was empty, as none of them could stand the smell any longer. So, after a good cleaning, it was given to the first Earl of Mouseton by King Stilton II as a reward for his support in the War of the Fondues. Roquefort, the present Lord Mouseton, is the 18th earl.

Over the centuries, the house has been greatly enlarged. In 1525, they added a west wing. In 1528, they added an east wing. (And in 1530, it tried to fly away.) Since then, various earls and countesses have added galleries and gazebos, towers and turrets, walled gardens, sunken ponds, stables, libraries, drawing rooms, conservatories . . . so many additions, in fact, that no one knows how many rooms the building has any more. Someone did try counting all the rooms once, but gave up at 314½.

That is why the house contains so many secrets and so many adventures – and why there is no such thing as an ordinary day at Mouseton Abbey.

WENSLEYDALE
Butler

MISS SWISS
Housekeeper

MRS. CHESHIRE
Cook

RACLETTE
Housemaid

MONTEREY JACK
Footman

MISS PARMESAN
Governess

ROQUEFORT,
EARL OF MOUSETON

People call him Lord Mouseton.

LADY BRIE,
COUNTESS OF MOUSETON

Lord Mouseton's wife, also called Lady Mouseton.

LADY RICOTTA

Eldest daughter of
Lord and Lady Mouseton.

LADY MOZZARELLA

Second daughter of
Lord and Lady Mouseton.

LADY FONTINA

Youngest daughter of
Lord and Lady Mouseton.

LADY GOUDA,
DOWAGER COUNTESS OF MOUSETON

Lord Mouseton's mother.

GREAT UNCLE GORGONZOLA
and GREAT AUNT HALOUMI

Lord Mouseton's relatives, although no one's quite sure how.

Lord Mouseton is SUCH a forgetful mouse! He's always losing things. In the last month, he has lost two pairs of spectacles, his pocket watch, and his second-best pair of trousers. No one knows how he managed to lose these things (especially the trousers, since he was wearing them at the time).

Lady Brie bought him a planner for his birthday, so he could write down important dates. But he lost it.

Lord Mouseton was just sitting down to breakfast one morning when Lady Brie came in.

"Good morning, my dear," she said. "And a happy Cheesemas to you!"

"I am SUCH a forgetful mouse!" said Lord Mouseton. "I'd forgotten all about Cheesemas!" And then he said: "Goodness me! The family is coming! I must get everything ready."

And he rushed out.

"Oh, dear," said Lady Brie to the maid, Raclette. "He's forgotten to eat his breakfast!"

Lord Mouseton went to the Great Gallery
at the top of the house and there he saw before
him the Mouseton family's most precious
possession – the Great Big Cheesy Diamond.

Every Cheesemas, the Mouseton family has a banquet. Great Uncle Gorgonzola comes all the way from Bavaria, Great Aunt Haloumi comes all the way from Bulgaria, and Lady Gouda, Lord Mouseton's mother, comes all the way from her rooms at the other end of the house.

At the end of the banquet, everyone gets a chance to hold the diamond and make a wish, and they all sing the traditional Mouseton Cheesemas song:

"Cheesy Diamond, shining bright, make my wish come true this night!"

(There are 96 more verses, but they don't sing those.)

Of course, the wishes only come true if the diamond is really, really SHINY.

So Lord Mouseton removed the diamond from its case, put it in his pocket, and took it downstairs to be cleaned by Wensleydale, the butler.

Or he meant to. But Mouseton Abbey is a big house, and Lord Mouseton is SUCH a forgetful mouse, that before he knew it, he was horribly lost.

Eventually, he saw a door he recognized, said "AHA!" in a purposeful way, and marched right through.

But it was the schoolroom, where his daughters were just starting their lessons. Lord Mouseton tripped over one of their schoolbags and knocked over a desk. Books and papers went everywhere.

a b c d e f
g h i j k l
m n o p q r
s t u v w x
y z cat

"Father!" said Ricotta.

"Daddy!" said Mozzarella.

"Papa!" said Fontina.

"Oh, dear!" said Miss Parmesan,
their governess. "I've only just cleaned up!"

"Oh, er, yes . . ." said Lord Mouseton.
"Sorry about that. Excellent work. Keep going."

Then he looked around.

"Oh, and does anyone know the quickest
way downstairs?"

"We'll show you!" yelled the children.
"We know a REALLY quick way!"

And they took their father to the
Grand Staircase . . .

. . . where they all slid down
the bannisters!

At the bottom, they zoomed off the
bannisters and landed in a heap.

"Look out!" said Ricotta.

"Oops!" said Mozzarella.

"Weeee!" said Fontina.

"Oof!" said Lord Mouseton. "Well, at
least we landed on a nice, soft mattress."

"That's not a mattress," said Raclette,
the maid, who was standing nearby.
"That's Miss Swiss!"

They had landed on Miss Swiss, the housekeeper!

"Oh, I do beg your pardon," said Lord Mouseton.

Miss Swiss was quite angry.

"Please, my lord," she said, "I am trying to get everything clean for the guests. It is very difficult to clean things properly when people use the bannisters as if they were a ride at the funfair!"

"Oh, er, yes, of course . . ." said Lord Mouseton. "Sorry about that. Excellent work. Keep going."

And they hurried into the kitchen.

In the kitchen, Mrs. Cheshire, the cook, was preparing the Cheesemas banquet. She was stirring the mixture for her famous Cheesemas pudding. She serves this every Cheesemas, and it is Lord Mouseton's favorite.

"Oooh," he said. "Can I have a little taste?"

"No, you may not, milord!" said Mrs. Cheshire. "I'm just adding all the spices."

"Oh," said Lord Mouseton. "I'll just have a sniff then."

And he sniffed the pudding. But all the flour and the spices got up his nose . . .

"Ahhh . . . ahhh . . . CHOOOO!"

Flour went everywhere. Raisins went everywhere. Cheese went everywhere.

"Out you go!" yelled Mrs. Cheshire. "Look at the mess!"

"Oh, er, yes, of course . . ." said Lord Mouseton. "Sorry about that. Excellent work. Keep going."

And they hurried into the butler's pantry.

In the butler's pantry, Wensleydale, the butler, and Monterey Jack, the footman, were waiting.

"Ah, Wensleydale," said Lord Mouseton. "Do you have everything?"'

"Yes, my lord," replied Wensleydale.

"You have the brushes? And the cloths? And the special cleaner?"

"Yes, my lord," said Wensleydale.

"Good. Well done. Excellent work. Keep going."

"There is one thing still missing," said Wensleydale.

"What is it?"

"The Great Big Cheesy Diamond, my lord."

"Oh, er, yes, of course," said Lord Mouseton.
"I am SUCH a forgetful mouse! I have it right here."

He felt in his pocket. But the diamond wasn't there.

"Oh. Must be in the other pocket."

But it wasn't. The diamond wasn't in any
of Lord Mouseton's pockets.

In fact, the diamond was missing!

"We must find it!" cried Lord Mouseton. "Hurry!"

They hurried back into the kitchen and started searching.

"NO!" yelled Mrs. Cheshire. "I can't manage with all this disruption!"

"But this is an EMERGENCY!" said Lord Mouseton. "Don't just stand there – come and help!"

They looked in pots and pans. They looked in buckets and bowls. They looked in the pantry, in the sink, and even under Mrs. Cheshire's hat.

They searched and searched, but there was no sign of the diamond. (Although they did find both pairs of Lord Mouseton's missing spectacles.)

So they hurried to the Grand Staircase . . .

. . . where they ran straight into Miss Swiss.

"Oh, no!" she cried. "Not again!"

"This is a CRISIS!" said Lord Mouseton. "Come and help!"

They looked in vases and urns. They looked in potted plants and under furniture. They looked in the umbrella stand and under the carpet, and even in Miss Swiss's pockets.

They searched and searched, but there was no sign of the diamond. (Although they did find Lord Mouseton's lost pocket watch.)

So they hurried to the schoolroom . . .

. . . where Miss Parmesan had just finished cleaning up.

"Oh, my goodness!" she said. "I've just finished clearing up the mess!"

"This is a DISASTER!" said Lord Mouseton. "Come and help!"

They looked in schoolbooks and pencil cases. They looked in the paint pots and under the blackboard. They looked in the desks and in the schoolbags, and even behind the big map of the world.

They searched and searched, but there was no sign of the diamond. (Although they did find the planner that Lady Brie had given Lord Mouseton for his birthday.)

So they hurried to the Great Gallery . . .

. . . where Lady Brie had come
to see what all the fuss was about.

"Do calm down, dear," she said.
"You'll have one of your headaches."

"But this is a CATASTROPHE!" said
Lord Mouseton. "Come and help."

They looked on the shelves and
behind the paintings. They looked
in the candlesticks and inside
the clock. They looked on the
mantelpiece and under the rugs,
and even on the chandelier.

They searched and searched, but there was no sign of the diamond. (Although they did find Lord Mouseton's second-best pair of trousers. How they got there, nobody knows.)

The Great Big Cheesy Diamond was completely lost!

"It's useless!" wailed Lord Mouseton. "I have let down the entire family. The diamond has gone, and that means nobody gets to make their Cheesemas wish!"

At the Cheesemas banquet that night,
Lord Mouseton didn't laugh or smile.
He didn't tell any of his silly jokes.
He scarcely listened to all the news from
Bavaria, or the stories from Bulgaria.

"Where is the diamond?" asked Lady Gouda in a very loud voice.

"Oh, er, um," said Lord Mouseton. "Well, Mother, we thought we might have a change this year."

"Eh?" said Lady Gouda (who was very deaf). "You think it might rain in my ear?"

"No! I mean we thought it was time for something new."

"Some stew? I don't want any stew. We don't have stew at Cheesemas. We have Cheesemas pudding."

At that very moment, Wensleydale arrived.

"My lords and ladies," he said. "The Cheesemas pudding is served!"

Lord Mouseton was so upset, he didn't even want any Cheesemas pudding.

"Come along, dear," said Lady Brie. "It's your favorite."

"What's the point?" said Lord Mouseton. "The whole thing is RUINED."

"Yes, dear," said Lady Brie. "But we don't have to be hungry as well, do we?"

So Lord Mouseton tasted a spoonful. And it was yummy. He took another spoonful and it was even more yummy.

Then he had another spoonful and it was . . .
"Owwwww!"

He had bitten on something really hard.
He spat it out.

There, in his plate, was the diamond!

"I've found the Great Big Cheesy
Diamond!" he cried. "But how on
earth did it get in the pudding?"

"I know, Papa," said Fontina.
"It must have fallen into the pudding
mixture when you sniffed the spices
and sneezed!"

So they passed the diamond around and everyone made a wish.

And everyone sang the traditional Mouseton Cheesemas song:

"Cheesy Diamond, shining bright,
    make my wish come true this night!"

(Great Uncle Gorgonzola wanted to sing the other 96 verses,
but he was overruled.)

Everyone said that they had never seen the Great Big Cheesy Diamond looking so shiny and sparkly and bright.

"Excellent," said Lord Mouseton. "Do you know, it looks so lovely, I think I'm going to clean it with Mrs. Cheshire's Cheesemas Pudding mix every year!"

The End.